Going Up!

Martin Waddell

illustrated by Russell Ayto

WALKER BOOKS
AND SUBSIDIARIES
LONDON • BOSTON • SYDNEY

Going Up

My name is Jackie D. I play for Belton Goalbusters with my mates Farouk and Dipper.

Our video diary shows the big games in our fight for promotion from the

Holt Boys' League Third Division,
the very first year we were in it.

Dipper's dad filmed our big games
so we could see ourselves on TV.

This is how the Holt Boys' League Third Division table looked before we played our first game against Owen United.

We stuck the league table up in our football hut and Dipper said it was brilliant because it showed us as top of the league.

"It is only alphabetical," I told him. "We haven't played any games yet."

"I know that," said Dipper. "But it still makes us top of the league!"

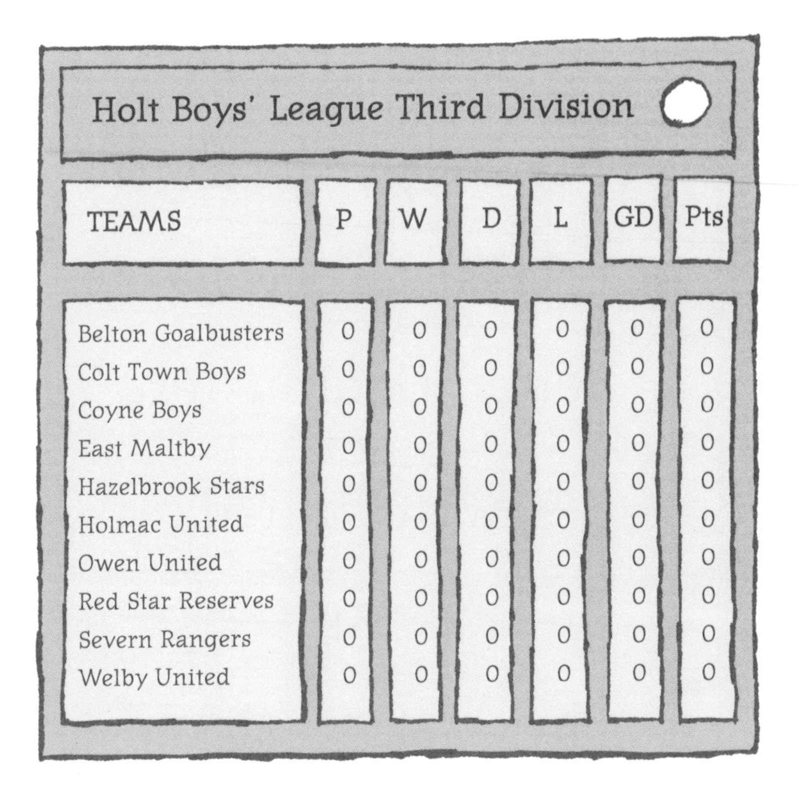

Holt Boys' League Third Division

TEAMS	P	W	D	L	GD	Pts
Belton Goalbusters	0	0	0	0	0	0
Colt Town Boys	0	0	0	0	0	0
Coyne Boys	0	0	0	0	0	0
East Maltby	0	0	0	0	0	0
Hazelbrook Stars	0	0	0	0	0	0
Holmac United	0	0	0	0	0	0
Owen United	0	0	0	0	0	0
Red Star Reserves	0	0	0	0	0	0
Severn Rangers	0	0	0	0	0	0
Welby United	0	0	0	0	0	0

Game one in the league! Our first ever game.

This is Jonathan Tew saving.

This is Jonathan throwing the ball out to Dipper.

This is me, Jackie D, going near post.

This is Farouk, at the far post.

This is Dipper White, chipping the ball.

This is me, scoring our first ever goal on TV.

This is our very first goal celebration!

This is Farouk heading our second goal.

This is Farouk poaching another.

This is me putting Dipper through the middle.

This is Dipper outpacing their stopper.

This is their goalie trying to trip Dipper.

This is Dipper putting the ball in the net.

It was our very first game in the league, and we WON 4–1.

Dipper's dad missed their goal because they scored after only three minutes, and he was still finding out how the camera worked.

When we won 4–1 against Owen, that made us third in the league, because of goal difference and other teams winning.

Holt Boys' League Third Division

TEAMS	P	W	D	L	GD	Pts
Welby United	1	1	0	0	+7	3
Hazelbrook Stars	1	1	0	0	+5	3
Belton Goalbusters	1	1	0	0	+3	3
Holmac United	1	1	0	0	+2	3
East Maltby	1	1	0	0	+2	0

League game six, against our big local rivals.

This is me, almost scoring.

This is Farouk heading the ball into the net ... but he was offside.

This is Jonathan punching clear.

This is Jonathan saving again.

This is Dipper getting himself yellow-carded.

This is Welby scoring. 0–1.

We LOST 0–1. It was our home game, so our score comes first.

"Now we won't win the league!" Farouk said afterwards in the changing-room.

"We still might," Dipper told him. "We've only lost one out of six. We've still got twelve to play."

It was the first game we had lost in our fight for promotion.

Holt Boys' League Third Division

TEAMS	P	W	D	L	GD	Pts
East Maltby	6	6	0	0	+15	18
Welby United	6	6	0	0	+12	18
Hazelbrook Stars	6	6	0	0	+10	18
Belton Goalbusters	6	5	0	1	+14	15

League game number nine,
playing the team at the top!

Farouk scored our first goal. 0–1.

Our second goal in three minutes – scored by JD! (That's me.) 0–2.

Dipper scored! 0–3 to us!

Our centre-back, Mojo, scored one from a corner. 0–4.

Their centre-back scored an own goal.

0–5.

Dipper's dad mucked it up. He missed one more goal scored by yours truly – me.

That made it 0–6 to us. Big, big, big, brilliant win for the Goalbusters, against the best team in the league. We were on our way to promotion!

"Our goalie had flu!" their coach told us.

Holt Boys' League Third Division

TEAMS	P	W	D	L	GD	Pts
East Maltby	10	9	0	1	+16	27
Welby United	9	8	1	0	+18	25
Belton Goalbusters	9	8	0	1	+19	24

League game number ten, against a big team with Farouk's brother in it.

We scored an own goal. 1–0.

Then I laid one on for Dipper – 1–1.

And then ...

Dipper laid one on for me. That made it 1–2.

Farouk got another: 1–3. That was almost the end of the scoring.

This is Jonathan Tew saving their spot kick.

This is me missing a sitter.

This is Hazelbrook getting their second goal. That made it 2–3.

We were top of the league, with ten games played and eight games to go.

"Looks like it will be between Welby, East Maltby and us!" Farouk said, on the bus home after the game. "Two will go up, and the other stays down."

That's when things went wrong.

Dipper's mum took him off to Scotland to see his old auntie. So we played Welby again without Dipper. I led the line with Farouk in behind, but it didn't work.

We drew it 0–0, which meant Welby had taken four points from two games against us, and we'd taken one.

That was bad enough, but we lost the next two games 0–1 and 1–3. Then we won 2–1, and drew the next one. That left us fourth in the table, with three games to go.

Holt Boys' League Third Division

TEAMS	P	W	D	L	GD	Pts
East Maltby	15	11	2	2	+18	35
Hazelbrook Stars	17	11	1	5	+8	34
Welby United	15	11	1	3	+16	34
Belton Goalbusters	15	10	2	3	+12	32

League game number 16. We had to win it or we'd miss out on promotion.

Farouk scored. 1–0.

Dipper got one. 2–0.

JD got a smash-bang-wallop-brilliant goal. 3–0.

I made a goal for Mickey Dejong, who came on when Dipper was hurt. 4–0.

"How did that team draw with Welby?" I asked Farouk down at his dad's cafe.

"Doesn't matter!" said Farouk. "What we have to do now is keep winning our games."

And we did it. East Maltby lost twice in a week, and then Welby lost again. We were level with Welby with one game to go. We both drew 2–2 in our last league games.

That left the final league like this:

Holt Boys' League Third Division

TEAMS	P	W	D	L	GD	Pts
Welby United	18	12	3	3	+22	39
Belton Goalbusters	18	12	3	3	+22	39
East Maltby	18	12	2	4	+10	38

"Goal difference the same! We will finish either second or first, so that means we're promoted," Dipper said, when we stuck the league table up in our football hut. "We have to play off with Welby to win the league title!"

It was the BIGGEST big game for the Goalbusters, ever!

The biggest big game that we played!

First goal scored just after the kick-off ...

goalscorer: JD! 0–1.

They scored and made it 1–1.

We had our team talk at half-time.

Farouk scored with a header. That made it 1–2 to us.

They scored again. That made it 2–2.

FULL TIME. 2–2.

This is Farouk blazing wide in extra time.

The ref blew! It was down to penalty kicks.

They scored. 1–0.

Then we scored. 1–1.

Then they scored. 2–1.

We scored. 2–2.

They missed. 2–2.

We missed. 2–2.

They scored. 3–2.

We scored too. 3–3.

They missed again! Still 3–3, with the final kick to come.

It was up to me. I had to take the kick that could win Goalbusters the title!

This is me winning the league for the Goalbusters.

WE WON IT! cheered Farouk.

That's how Belton Goalbusters FC won the title. It was the first ever year that we played in the league.

Top goal-scorers: Farouk and me!

For Paul
M.W.
For Phillip and Stephen
R.A.

Walker Starters

The Dragon Test by June Crebbin, illustrated by Polly Dunbar
0-7445-9018-3
Hal the Highwayman by June Crebbin, illustrated by Polly Dunbar
0-7445-9019-1
Cup Run by Martin Waddell, illustrated by Russell Ayto
0-7445-9026-4
Going Up! by Martin Waddell, illustrated by Russell Ayto
0-7445-9027-2
Big Wig by Colin West
0-7445-9017-5
Percy the Pink by Colin West
0-7445-9054-X

Series consultant: Jill Bennett, author of
Learning to Read with Picture Books

First published 2003 by
Walker Books Ltd
87 Vauxhall Walk
London SE11 5HJ

10 9 8 7 6 5 4 3

This book has been typeset in Journal Text

Printed in China

British Library Cataloguing in Publication Data:
a catalogue record for this book is available from the British Library

ISBN 0-7445-9027-2

www.walkerbooks.co.uk